Walt Disney's

Ben and Me

* * * ★ * * *

If you should ever visit the fair city of Philadelphia, very likely you will see a fine statue of Benjamin Franklin—philosopher, inventor, patriot, and one of our country's first great leaders.

And if you are fortunate enough to have a good view of the crown of the statue's hat, you may see there a tiny statue of one Amos Mouse. It was Amos, you see, who was really responsible for many of the great deeds credited to Ben Franklin.

Here is the story in Amos's own words:

I was born and raised in Philadelphia, in the old church on Second Street, and, yes, I was as poor as a church mouse. There were twenty-six children in my family. Since I was the oldest, I decided to set out into the world and make my own way.

It was the winter of 1745. Jobs were scarce, especially for a mouse. All day I tramped through the snow. By nightfall, I did  not know where to turn. My last hope was an old run-down shop at the edge of town. A sign over the door read BENJ. FRANKLIN, PRINTER & BOOKBINDER.

I found my way inside. The place was cold and dark and full of strange contraptions. In the shadows sat a

round-faced man, trying to write by candlelight.

Suddenly, he sneezed: "Ah—*choo!*" Off flew his glasses. They crashed to the floor and broke!

"Oh, don't tell me!" cried the man, picking up his broken glasses. "My last pair! Now I'll never get this issue of my newspaper finished! It's hopeless."

"But you can't give up!" I told him. "Nothing ventured, nothing gained, Mr. Franklin!"

"My name's Ben," he said. "And who might you be?"

I introduced myself and before long, it was clear that Ben needed me around. I

helped him build a stove to warm his shop, and I fixed his glasses. He had broken both his outdoor pair and his reading pair. The only thing left to do was to make one pair out of the two.

So I fit the pieces of glass together as best I could.

"Why, Amos!" he cried, when he tried them on.

"They're great! Two-way glasses! Bifocals, we'll call them." And if you know your history, of course you know that bifocals became famous.

I also helped Ben finish the latest issue of his

newspaper and gave him tips to make it more interesting.

By evening the next day, everyone in Philadelphia was

reading it.

From then on I went everywhere with Ben, riding conveniently on his hat.

Well, the years went by, and Ben's reputation grew. Letters poured in from people all over the colonies. They asked his advice on all kinds of things. It took most of my spare time to answer them all.

Yours,
Amos

Meanwhile, Ben puttered around with his experiments. And it was one of them that led us at last to the parting of our ways. At first, he fussed around with sparks and jars with wires in them. He said he was studying electricity.

Then Ben took up kite flying. To the framework of his largest kite, he fastened a small box just for me. He said I was to be the world's first flying reporter.

I was so thrilled by flying that I failed to notice a sharp, pointed wire fastened to the kite above my head.

The first hint I had that anything was wrong was when the sky darkened with thunderclouds and a mean rain began to blow. The kite spun and shivered, but Ben would not pull me in!

I screamed myself hoarse. I tugged at the rope. Now lightning was flashing along the horizon. Thunder rolled. The storm was moving our way. Suddenly, lightning struck my kite! The shock went through me and almost tore the kite to ribbons.

Now—too late—Ben began to wind in his rope. The kite and I slowly descended and landed in a tree. When Ben found us there, he scooped me up in one hand.

"Amos! Amos! Speak to me!" he cried. "Was it electricity?"

I couldn't believe it! All he cared about was whether or not the sizzle in a lightning bolt was the same as electricity! That was the end for me!

"Good-bye, forever!" I said. He pleaded with me to change my mind, but I left Ben and went back to my family in the old church.

The years that followed were troubled ones. Restless

crowds filled the streets. There were riots as well as

loud talk against the stamp tax and other taxes for the

British king. Ben was chosen to go to England and lay

our case before the king.

The colonies eagerly awaited his return. But his mission was a failure. The king would not listen. It seemed as if war would surely come. But the people had no clear statement of their cause to hold them together. I heard that poor Ben was worried.

I could help him—I knew I could. But no! I could not go back. After all, a mouse has his pride!

Then, one night in 1776, I was awakened by a voice. Sleepily, I peered through the mouse hole. There, on bended knee, was Ben Franklin himself.

"Amos, I'm here to ask you to come back," he said humbly.

I was pleased and touched, but I did not let him see it.

"I have big decisions to make," Ben continued, "and I can't make them alone. You just must come back."

"On my own terms?" I asked. "If I draw up an agreement, will you sign it?"

"I'll sign anything," he vowed.

So back I went, having spent the night writing the agreement by candlelight.

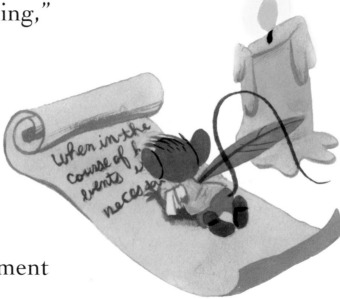

Ben was glad to see me the next morning, you may be sure. I gave him my agreement to sign at once.

That was

when a knock

came at the

door. It was

Thomas

Jefferson. He

was one of

the leaders of

the colonies, too, and Ben called him "Red." He was

writing a statement about what the colonists believed

in—a Declaration of Independence.

But, struggle as he would, Red could not get the beginning right.

"'The time has come—'" Red began to read, but then he stopped. "No, Ben, it isn't right. 'The time is at hand'...no...."

"Psst, Ben!" I said, when I saw how upset Red was. "How about our contract?"

"Shh!" said Ben. "Just a minute."

"No," I insisted. "Now!"

So Ben began to read the contract aloud: "'When in the course of human events, it becomes necessary—'"

"Ben!" cried Red Jefferson. "That's it! That's it!"

So that's how it happened that I supplied the beginning for the Declaration of Independence. Oh, I didn't get credit, of course. But fame doesn't matter to a mouse. I have my memories of the good old days and Ben and me.

WALT DISNEY's
GOOFY,
Movie Star

Once upon a time there was a wonderful place called Hollywood. It was the center of Movie Land.

Everyone in Hollywood, it seemed, wanted to be a movie star.

Every waitress was waiting to be discovered so she could be a movie star. And every young man working in a filling station planned to be one,

too. They were all waiting for a talent scout to come along and change their lives. For a talent scout, you know, is a person who finds new movie stars.

Driving down the streets of Hollywood, you knew at once you were in Movie Land. You almost wanted to be a movie star yourself.

There was just one person in Hollywood, it seemed, who didn't care to be a movie star. His name was Dippy Dog, and he was a happy soul.

Dippy liked the movies, of course. He liked to sit in the balcony of the theater with some popcorn and see a picture show.

"*Yuk, yuk, yuk!*" He would laugh his merry laugh. And everyone around would laugh with him.

One night at the movie theater, some talent scouts heard Dippy laugh. "Who is that laughing?" they cried. "He has the makings of a movie star!" And when they found out it was Dippy Dog, the talent scouts hustled him off to a movie studio.

Soon Dippy was about to sign a contract to be a movie star.

"What's your name, son?" asked the producer. "Dippy Dog? That will never do! We need a name that breathes romance: Dandy — Daffy — *Goofy*! That's it!"

So Goofy signed his new name to the contract. And then he was a movie star.

Now Goofy had to dress like a movie star. He had whole closets full of fancy clothes.

And he had to have some shiny new cars—not just one new car, but four!

He had to move from his little house to a mansion worthy of a star.

And Goofy had to have his picture taken, of course. He had his picture taken waking up, eating his breakfast—even brushing his teeth.

He had his picture taken dressed for golf and tennis and hopscotch and polo.

Goofy was so busy having pictures taken for newspapers and magazines and television shows that he had to make a special appointment to play.

He even had pictures taken for a movie. He was the star, of course.

Now whenever he went to eat in a restaurant, movie fans waited at the door to see him walk in and out.

The night his movie opened, all the pretty girls and handsome young men who wanted to be movie stars also lined up outside the theater.

"Isn't he wonderful?" they said. "How did he do it?"

Then along came a famous newspaper writer to interview the new star. "What is the secret of your success?" she asked.

"*Yuk, yuk, yuk!*" Goofy laughed the laugh that made him famous. "I guess I just have fun, that's all."

And that is the story of how Goofy became a movie star in Hollywood, once upon a time.

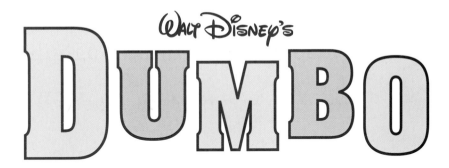

Walt Disney's DUMBO

It was spring—
spring in the circus!
After the long winter's
rest, it was time to
set out again on the
open road.

"Toot! Toot!"
whistled Casey Jones,
the locomotive of the
circus train, and the
circus was on its way!

Inside the elephant car, a stork had just delivered Mrs. Jumbo's baby. And a darling baby elephant he was, too. One of the grown-up elephants tickled him under his chin. The tickling made him sneeze. And when he sneezed, out flapped his ears — the most enormous ears any of them had ever seen!

All the grown-up elephants laughed. "He'll never be a Little Jumbo," they said. "Little *Dumbo* is the name for him!"

Poor little Dumbo toddled to his mother, and she tenderly rocked him to sleep.

Before dawn, Casey Jones brought the train to

a stop in the city where the circus was to open. After

the tents were set up, there was a big parade down

the main street: horses, acrobats, lions in their

wagon-cages, and, last but not least, the elephants

marching slowly in single file.

At the end of the line came Dumbo, and all went well until the crowd caught sight of his ears.

"He can't be an elephant!" they cried. "He must be a clown!"

Dumbo tried
to walk faster. But
he stumbled and
tripped on his
ears. Down he
went in a puddle
of mud. The

crowd roared with laughter.

Later, at the circus grounds, some boys gathered in
front of Dumbo and Mrs. Jumbo. One boy grabbed
Dumbo's ear and pulled it—hard.

Mrs. Jumbo would not stand for that! She snatched the boy up with her trunk, dropped him across the rope, and spanked him.

"Help, help!" cried the boy, and the keepers came running. Soon Mrs. Jumbo was behind bars in the prison wagon with a big sign that said DANGER! MAD ELEPHANT!

Poor Dumbo. He missed his mother, and the other elephants would have nothing to do with him. Little Timothy, the circus mouse, was his only friend. Timothy wanted to help Dumbo find a special use for those special ears and become famous!

Timothy helped

Dumbo practice

springboard

jumping so that

he could jump

atop the pyramid

of elephants at

the end of the

show. But when

the big moment came, Dumbo tripped over his ears

and knocked over the elephant pyramid.

That did it. The next day, they made Dumbo into a clown. He had to jump from the top of a blazing cardboard house, down into the clown-firemen's net.

But Timothy would not give up. "We'll have you starring yet," Timothy whispered to Dumbo. "You'll be flying high."

Back in the circus tent, with Timothy curled up in his hat brim, Dumbo drifted off to sleep and dreamed a beautiful dream. In it, he was the star of a magical circus. He stepped onto a springboard, bounced high into the air — and then away he flew.

It seemed as easy as anything, and very, very real.

The next morning, Timothy was the first to awaken. He was still in the brim of Dumbo's hat, and the hat was still on Dumbo's head. But Dumbo was asleep on the branch of a tree, far above the ground!

"You and that elephant just came flying up," some crows said to Timothy.

"Flying?" yelled Timothy.

Dumbo opened his eyes, tried to stand up, and fell out of the tree.

"Dumbo!" cried Timothy. "If you can fly when you're asleep, you can fly when you're awake." So

Dumbo tried again

. . . and again. . . .

But he could not

leave the ground.

At last the

crows felt sorry for

him. "Here, try

this magic feather,"

one of them said. "Hold on to this, and you'll be fine."

Dumbo clutched the feather in his trunk and tried

once more. It worked! Up into the air he soared like a bird. He glided, he dipped, he dove. The crows cheered.

Timothy cheered, too, as he and Dumbo headed back to the circus grounds. They decided to keep Dumbo's flying a secret—a surprise for the afternoon show.

So Dumbo and
Timothy waited inside
the cardboard house all
through the show, until
the make-believe fire
crackled up around
them. Then Timothy
tucked the magic
feather into Dumbo's
trunk, and climbed into
Dumbo's hat brim.

Down below, the clown-firemen brought a big net, held it out, and Dumbo jumped!

But as he jumped, the feather slipped from his trunk. Now his magic was gone, Dumbo thought. He began to plunge like a stone.

Timothy saw the feather drift away. Thinking quickly, he shouted, "The feather was a trick! You can fly by yourself!"

Doubtfully, Dumbo spread his ears wide—and swooped up into the air!

The audience roared with delight. Dumbo was flying!

In that instant, everything changed for Dumbo. The keepers freed Mrs. Jumbo and brought her into the tent to see her baby fly. Soon Dumbo was a

hero from coast to coast. Timothy became his manager and saw to it that Dumbo got a wonderful contract with a big salary and a pension for his mother.

And the circus was even renamed "Dumbo's Flying Circus" in honor of the elephant with the very special ears and a very special talent.

Walt Disney's Pecos Bill

* * * ★ * * *

Down Texas way, the Pecos River flows. Where it comes from, no one knows!

One day, a long time back, when a prairie wagon full of children, dogs, pots, and pans was crossing the Pecos River, the smallest child just rolled right out the back!

That child's name was Bill. He sat there all alone on the prairie until a mother coyote came along and took pity on him. She decided to take him home and raise him as her own, along with her coyote pups.

Bill felt right at home with the coyotes— and with all the other animals out on the prairie. He was spunky, too. As Bill grew, he learned how to out-lope the antelopes, out-jump the jackrabbits, and out-hiss the snakes!

Then one day, a young colt wandered into the Pecos

land. The poor thing was weak and couldn't defend himself against the buzzards. So Bill decided to help him out. Before long, Bill had taken care of those buzzards, and Bill and the colt were friends.

From then on, those two stuck together like warts

on a toad. As Bill grew, he became a cowboy—the

"toughest critter west of the Alamo!" His weak, little

colt grew into a big, strong horse known as Widowmaker,

because he had bucked off so many cowboys.

Why, the two of them became famous in the Pecos

land, and
their deeds
even more
so. Bill
could rope
anything
with his
lariat —

even a raging cyclone. He straddled it, then tamed it to

a breeze.

When there was a drought all over Texas, Bill lassoed

and towed a rain cloud from California to wet things down. That's how we got the Gulf of Mexico!

And when a group of cattle rustlers stole Bill's herd, he caught the villains and  knocked out all their fillings. That's the reason we have gold in them thar hills!

Once, Bill lost his way in the desert. He knew he'd

never make it across without some water. So he got a stick and dug the Rio Grande as he went!

Through it all, Widowmaker was always at Bill's side. It looked as though nothing would ever come

between Bill and his horse.

Then along came Sluefoot Sue, the first woman Bill had ever seen.

To Widowmaker, Sue looked like trouble. And sure enough, she was, for Bill and Sue soon fell in love.

Sue wanted to marry Bill, and she wanted to do it while riding Widowmaker. Well, that  horse was not about to stand for it. The cowhands brought him over to her, fit to be tied! That didn't bother Sue. She climbed right on Widowmaker's back.

The more that horse bucked and reared, the tighter she

hung on. She was a
real bronc rider!

The only
problem was that
Sue was wearing a
wire bustle under
her wedding dress.

Little by little, that bustle began to act as a spring as she

bounced up and down, each time sending her higher

and higher
into the air.
Then,
suddenly, the
reins snapped
and Sue went
flying skyward!

Well, Bill got out his lariat and swung it in a wide loop. Hadn't he lassoed everything from a cyclone to a gang of rustlers? Surely, he could lasso Sue and bring her back down to earth.

He threw the loop wide and high up in the sky. But for the first time in his life . . . Bill missed. No one could understand it, except Widowmaker. He was standing on the rope!

Sue kept on flying right up to the moon,

and that was where she stayed for all time. As for Bill,

he rode away from the plains and never returned.

Folks think he went back to the coyotes. They say

that when the coyotes howl at the full moon, you can

hear Bill howling right along with them.

But just ask anyone today who the best cowboy in Texas is. They'll still tell you it's Pecos Bill!

"I've had such fun today, Mickey!" exclaimed Minnie Mouse. "There's so much to do here at Walt Disney World—the rides, the shops, the movies . . . and, of course, the yummy snacks!"

"I had fun, too," Mickey said. "And I can't wait to lead the parade tonight! I'll get to wear my brand-new drum major's hat. I have it right—oh, no!"

Mickey's hat was missing!

"I had it with me all day," said Mickey. "I must have left it someplace."

"I'll help you look for it," Minnie said. "Come on. Our last stop was Space Mountain," she added as they headed back to the ride.

Mickey and Minnie held on as the ride swooped around high-speed curves. "Wow! What a ride!" said Mickey. "But I don't see my hat."

Mickey and Minnie found their friend Donald Duck at their next stop—the Grand Prix Raceway.

"I haven't seen your hat," Donald said as he sped away. "But I just saw Goofy, and he was wearing a new hat."

Mickey and Minnie searched all over Tomorrowland for the missing hat. "Let's catch the Skyway," Minnie suggested.

Soon they were floating high above Fantasyland. As they scanned the park below, it seemed to Mickey that everyone had a hat on. But he didn't see his own.

They bumped into Daisy Duck at It's a Small World and told her about the missing hat.

"I haven't seen it," Daisy said, "but I heard Goofy got a new hat today."

"Hmm," said Mickey. "That's what Donald said."

"Next stop, Frontierland," Minnie said.

"Gee, it would be fun to take a riverboat ride,"
Mickey said.

"We'll do that

next time!" said

Minnie. "For now,

we had better

check out Big

Thunder Mountain

Railroad." But

there was no sign of the hat there, either.

Minnie tried to reassure Mickey. "Don't worry," she said. "We'll find your hat." When they reached Liberty Square, Mickey spotted a hat outside the Hall of Presidents. But it

turned out to be Ben Franklin's, not Mickey's.

Before long, the search led Mickey and Minnie to the Pirates of the Caribbean ride in Adventureland, where they met up with Huey, Dewey, and Louie.

"Hi, boys," Mickey said. "Have you seen my new drum major's hat? I lost it somewhere in the Magic Kingdom."

"Nope," said Huey.

"But Goofy has a new hat," added Dewey.

"Yeah, it's really cool," finished Louie.

Mickey and Minnie went from shop to shop on Main Street. They still couldn't find Mickey's hat anywhere. Mickey was ready to give up his search. But there was one more place to look—the movie theater.

Just then, they spotted their friend, Goofy. He was carrying a *very* familiar object.

"My hat!" Mickey cried.

"It's yours?" Goofy exclaimed. "*Gawrsh*, I had no idea. I found it in the movie theater."

There once was a man named Paul Revere who went riding under the midnight moon for liberty, because he wanted a country without a king.

Who was this Paul Revere?

Paul Revere was a silversmith in old Boston town. If anything could be made of silver, Paul Revere could make it. In his shop on Fish Street, he made teapots and cream pots, buckles and bowls, and spoons and jugs and cups.

One April night, he left his shop and walked quickly through the streets, keeping away from the king's soldiers in their red coats. He soon met up with a man named Robert Newman.

"The king's soldiers march tonight," Paul Revere said. "They want to capture two

of our men. I am riding
to Lexington to give
the warning."

Robert Newman
nodded. "I know the
plan. I will show
lanterns from the

church tower to tell our men how the British go: one
if by land, and two if by sea."

"Show two lanterns," said Paul Revere. "The
redcoats are going by sea."

While Robert Newman started up the tower, Paul Revere hurried home. He put on his boots and riding

coat and said good-bye to his wife and children. To his oldest son, he said, "Now it's up to you to take care of things, for there's no telling if I will return."

Once again, Paul Revere went out into the night. With two friends, he headed to the riverbank where he had hidden a rowboat.

"My spurs!" he said. "I've forgotten them! How can I ride without them?"

Then he saw that his dog had followed him. He wrote a note to Mrs. Revere and tied it to the dog's collar.

"Home, boy!" he said. "Home—as fast as you can!"

The dog was back in a few minutes, and tied around his neck were the spurs.

Getting into the boat, Paul Revere and his friends began to row across the river. To reach Lexington, Paul Revere first had to sneak past the *Somerset,* one of the king's big ships. At any moment, Paul Revere expected to hear cannon fire or the shout of a ship's officer. But none came, and at last the rowboat touched shore.

Not far from shore, Paul Revere met some men. They led him to the house of Deacon John Larkin, a friend of Paul Revere's, and gave him a horse.

"You must be careful, sir," said one of the men. "There are redcoats on the road."

Then Paul Revere began riding, riding, riding for liberty. Past fields and meadows, past orchards and

farms, he

rode toward

Lexington.

Suddenly,

ahead of

him, he saw

two men on

horseback.

Their pistols gleamed in the moonlight. Redcoats!

One of the soldiers galloped toward him, and Paul Revere cut across a field. Near a swamp he suddenly turned aside. He smiled as the horse behind him crashed into the swamp, its hooves sinking into the mud.

Spurring his horse on, Paul Revere raced to another road. Riding, riding, riding, he came at last to Lexington. He warned Sam Adams and John Hancock that the soldiers were coming for them.

Then Paul Revere continued riding toward the village of Concord. At every house along the way, he shouted: "To arms! To arms! The redcoats are coming!"

Everywhere men reached for their rifles.

Church bells rang, and drums rolled— for the redcoats were coming,

and the time had arrived to fight for liberty.

The war went on for years. And when it was over, there was a new country—the United States of America. It was a country without a king, just as Paul Revere had wanted.

And Americans have never forgotten Paul Revere,

who rode for liberty under the midnight moon.

Walt Disney's

Pluto Pup Goes to Sea

"You see that dog up there? That dog's a hero!" Mickey Mouse told Pluto Pup one day. They were down at the town dock, standing beside an ocean liner. Up on the deck lay a huge dog, looking proud and staring out to sea.

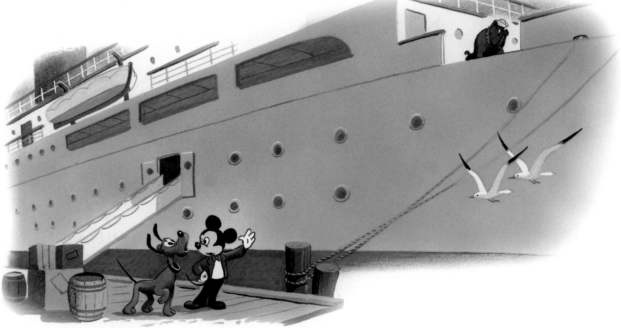

"There was a story in the paper about all the lives he's saved," said Mickey. "Wouldn't it be swell if you were a dog like that?"

Pluto thought, if all you had to do to be a hero was lie on a deck, staring out to sea, then he was willing to try it. The next gangplank they came to, up Pluto went.

Mickey did not miss him for a few minutes. Then he whistled and called and looked all around. But he could not find Pluto. High above, on the deck of a sleek white yacht, Pluto was sitting all alone, looking proud and haughty, and gazing out to sea.

No one on the yacht knew Pluto was on board until they had left the harbor for the open sea. Then the waves rose and fell, the yacht pitched and tossed, and Pluto was as unhappy as a dog can be.

Down below, the sailors shuddered at the dismal moans that came from the deck above. When they checked, they soon found the stowaway and led him to a corner of

the hold where they made him a bed of old rags.

"Too bad he doesn't

have sea legs," said the second mate to the first. "We could use a smart watchdog for the captain's jewels."

"Shh!" The first mate put a finger to his lips. "No one must know about those jewels!"

But it was too late. A tough-looking sailor had overheard the whole thing.

"Aha!" he said to himself. "Them jewels will line my pockets soon, and I'll jump ship at the very first port, or my name's not Pegleg Pete!"

The next day, Pluto felt much better. His nose led

him to the
galley, where the
ship's cat lived
with the cook.
Pluto heard the
cat hiss and he
took off for the
deck. The cat
came racing after

him so fast that, as the ship lurched, she slid across the

deck, under the rail, and down into the sea!

Pluto ran over for a better look—and skidded, with

a yelp, right after her!

After the sailors

rescued them, they

decided that Pluto

had jumped in to save

the cat. They called

him a hero and moved

his bed to the captain's cabin.

"He's just the dog we need to guard the captain's

jewels, after all," they said.

Pluto did not like being shut up in the cabin, though. He sent up such a howl that night that the captain shouted for the mates. "Take that mutt away. I'd rather be guarded *from* him than *by* him!" he cried.

So Pluto went back to his first spot on deck, looking proudly out to sea. He kept a sharp eye out for anyone about to fall overboard, because he liked the life of a hero.

That was the
night Pegleg
Pete had picked
to steal the
captain's jewels.
The ship lay
close to shore,
and Pete had

arranged for his friends to meet him with a boat. So
Pete slipped down to the cabin where the captain was
sound asleep and stole the jewels.

With the jewels safely stowed in a small leather pouch, Pegleg Pete signaled to his friends onshore. When they signaled back, he kicked off his shoe, and

dove over the rail into the water below. *Splash!* He started to swim for shore.

But Pluto had heard the splash. One of his friends must have fallen overboard, he thought. Time to be a hero again!

So Pluto jumped into the water, too.

"Man overboard!" the lookout yelled. The sailors turned the searchlight on and soon picked up Pluto and Pegleg Pete, bobbing in the water below.

Back on board, Pete quickly made up a story. "I saw the dear mutt slide in," he claimed. "I couldn't bear to think of anything happening to him, so I jumped in to save him, of course."

"Is that so?" said the first mate. "Then you won't mind showing me what's in that pouch!"

"I'll go get the captain!" the second mate cried, and ran off.

Pegleg Pete knew he was in big trouble. "Let me go!" he shouted, and he ran for the rail.

But Pluto did not want another bath in that cold water! He made a frantic jump for Pete's trousers and hung on to them!

Soon the second mate was back with the captain.

"Put Pete in the brig," the captain said. "And we'll get *you* a medal, sir," he said to Pluto the Pup.

So when the yacht came home at last, with Pluto sitting proudly up on deck, he was wearing the biggest, shiniest medal to be had. OUR HERO it said in gold.

Mickey was wandering down by the docks, as he did every lonely day, looking for his lost pup, when the yacht came into port.

"Arf!" cried Pluto, when he spotted Mickey.

"Pluto!" cried Mickey. "Where have you been? And look at that medal! What does it mean?"

The sailors told Mickey the whole tale.

"I guess you won't want to come back home, now that you're a ship's hero," Mickey said sadly.

In answer, Pluto gnawed his medal off his collar and laid it at Mickey's feet. He still thought the finest thing of all was to be Mickey Mouse's dog!

Walt Disney's
Paul Bunyan

Early one morning after a ferocious storm, a huge cradle washed up near a town in Maine. Inside the cradle was the biggest baby anyone had ever seen. The towns-folk adopted him and named him Paul Bunyan, because they thought it sounded like a big guy's name!

Paul grew into a good lad and everybody liked him.

He went to school just like all the other kids, but he was too big to fit inside the classroom.

So he sat outside and handed his lessons to the teacher by lifting the roof.

When school let out, all the kids would head for the old swimming hole. For huge Paul, it was more like a bathtub.

Paul was interested in a lot of things as a youngster. But as he got older and even bigger, he spent

more and more time out in the woods watching the loggers cut down trees. They cleared land so that farmers could plant crops, and they used the lumber to build new homes.

The townsfolk noticed Paul's fascination with logging, and one Christmas, they gave him a present that was to change his life forever and turn him into a legend. It was a great, big, beautiful ax—just the right size for Paul!

With that

big double-

bladed ax,

Paul could cut

down trees

faster than

most men could cut weeds. Wherever Paul logged, he

was followed by prospective farmers, for he could clear

enough land for a whole farm *in one day*.

But soon life in the East got too citified for Paul. So

he decided to head out west.

Soon winter came, and during one blizzard it was so cold that the snow itself turned blue! It was during this storm that Paul came upon a baby ox, frozen blue and shivering in the snow. Paul picked the ox up and held him close to thaw him out.

Even after he'd thawed out, the big ox stayed blue.

"I think I'll call you Babe," said Paul. "Babe the Blue Ox!"

Babe grew fast, and overnight he was twice as big as a barn. Paul thought it was great to have a pal as big as he was. So did Babe!

Babe became Paul's closest friend, and he was

mighty strong, too. One time, Paul set up a logging

 camp near a

river that had

too many bends

in it for logs to

float down. So

Paul tied one

end of a rope to Babe's yoke and anchored the other

end in the river.

Babe pulled that river straight as a pine log!

Paul and Babe kept moving westward. As they passed  through Minnesota, they got lost in a rainstorm. They wandered in circles for days. The big puddles left by their footprints remained full of water, and to this day folks still call Minnesota "the land of ten thousand lakes."

By summer's end, Paul and Babe had reached Wyoming. They were so glad to finally be out west that they got into a friendly wrestling match. They kicked up a whole mountain range, which is now called the Grand Tetons.

Out west, among the giant trees, there were big

logging camps that were just the kind of places for

Paul. Paul and Babe fit right in, with their hard work

and hearty appetites.

Then one day, a

stranger rolled into

camp aboard a shiny

new locomotive.

He walked right

up to a tree and began to cut it with a machine, the

likes of which no logger had ever seen!

"My name," said the stranger, "is Joe Muffaw, and I've got an automatic tree-cutting machine and a log-pulling locomotive that'll do your work in half the time."

Paul was angry. "Out here we use a double-bladed ax for cutting and oxen for pulling, little fella," he said.

Before long, a contest was organized to see who

could pull a triple load of logs faster: the locomotive or Babe the Blue Ox. Babe and the locomotive pulled with all their might, snorting and puffing. But when it was over, Babe had lost by just half an inch.

Sadly, Paul and Babe decided to say "so long" to their friends and head north.

Whatever happened to Paul Bunyan and Babe? Some folks say that logging machines put Paul out of business.

But others say that Paul went to Alaska, where the logging is endless and a man and his ox still have plenty of room.

Old Yeller

Nobody knew where Old Yeller came from. He just turned up one day at the Coateses' cabin, sniffing and snuffing and wagging his tail.

The Coates boys, Arliss and Travis, looked him over. Not that he was much to look at. He was big and clumsy and yellow in color.

He was full
of tricks, too.
Whenever
anyone picked
up a stick or a
stone, Old
Yeller threw
himself on the
ground. He
rolled around,
howling and yowling worse than a wildcat.

And he had to be watched. If he wasn't, he'd steal a person blind. Why, he could snatch a whole side of meat as slick as you please.

Old Yeller and Arliss took to each other right off. But Mrs. Coates wasn't sure if they should keep the dog. "If

your papa was here, he'd know what to do," she said.

But Mr. Coates was miles away, selling their steers in Abilene. He wouldn't be back for months. So Mrs. Coates told Arliss that Old Yeller could stay for the time being.

Whooping and hollering, Arliss ran for the pond, with Old Yeller right behind him.

Standing still, Old Yeller looked as though he couldn't walk without falling over his own feet. But when he started running, he was like a streak of lightning greased with hot bear oil. He was swift and sure and a sight to see.

He was so fast that he once caught a good-sized catfish in the pond for Arliss. Another time, he helped Travis drive some thieving raccoons out of the corn patch. And he was a wonder at herding cows or hogs.

Then one day, Arliss did something he shouldn't have and got himself into real trouble. He caught a bear cub

by the leg. And he wouldn't let go, not even when the big old mother bear came charging at him, snarling and growling.

Suddenly, from no place in particular, Old Yeller came bounding up. He tore right into that old bear.

And while Old Yeller fought the bear, Mrs. Coates and Travis came running and pulled Arliss away from the cub.

Soon the big bear had enough of the fighting and was running off through the brush with her cub. After he saw that Arliss was safe, Old Yeller wagged his tail.

"Oh, you crazy, wonderful old dog!" Mrs. Coates said. Now she was certain Old Yeller should stay.

But a few days later, a man came riding up to the cabin. His name was Sanderson, and he had lost a dog—a big yellow dog that was full of tricks. Old Yeller was his.

When Mr. Sanderson started to take Old Yeller away, Arliss shouted, "You can't have my  dog!" Mrs. Coates and Travis had to hold him back.

Mr. Sanderson looked at Arliss and then got down from his horse.

"Just a minute, young fellow," he said. "What's that in your pocket?"

"A horned toad," Arliss said, and held it out.

"Finest horned toad I ever saw," Mr. Sanderson said. Then, right then and there, Mr. Sanderson offered to swap his dog for Arliss's toad . . . if Mrs. Coates threw in a good home-cooked meal. Mrs. Coates smiled and nodded.

"All right. It's a swap," Mr. Sanderson said.

And so, Mr. Sanderson got a toad and a meal—and Arliss got Old Yeller.

"You're really my dog now, aren't you, boy?" Arliss said.

Old Yeller just wagged his tail and lay down in front of the fire. He knew he was there to stay.

Walt Disney's Casey at the Bat

The outlook wasn't brilliant for the Mudville nine that day:

The score stood four to two with but one inning more to play.

And then when Cooney died at first, and Barrows did the same,

A sickly silence fell upon the patrons of the game.

A straggling few got up to go in deep despair. The rest

Clung to that hope which springs eternal in the human breast;

They thought if only Casey could but get a whack at that—

We'd put up even money now, with Casey at the bat.

But Flynn preceded Casey, as did also Jimmy Blake,

And the former was a lulu and the latter was a cake;

So upon that stricken multitude grim melancholy sat,

For there seemed but little chance of Casey's getting to the bat.

But Flynn let drive a single, to the wonderment of all,

And Blake, the much despis-ed, tore the cover off the ball;

And when the dust had lifted, and the men saw what had occurred,

There was Jimmy safe at second and Flynn a-hugging third.

Then from five thousand throats and more there rose a lusty yell;

It rumbled through the valley, it rattled in the dell;

It knocked upon the mountain and recoiled upon the flat,

For Casey, mighty Casey, was advancing to the bat.

There was ease in Casey's manner as he stepped into his place;

There was pride in Casey's bearing and a smile on Casey's face.

And when, responding to the cheers, he lightly doffed his hat,

No stranger in the crowd could doubt 'twas Casey at the bat.

Ten thousand eyes were on him as he rubbed his hands with dirt;

Five thousand tongues applauded when he wiped them on his shirt.

Then while the writhing pitcher ground the ball into his hip,

Defiance gleamed in Casey's eye, a sneer curled Casey's lip.

And now the leather-covered sphere came hurtling through the air,

And Casey stood a-watching it in haughty grandeur there.

Close by the sturdy batsman the ball unheeded sped—

"That ain't my style," said Casey. "Strike one," the umpire said.

From the benches, black with people, there went up a muffled roar,

Like the beating of the storm-waves on a stern and distant shore.

"Kill him! Kill the umpire!" shouted someone on the stand;

And it's likely they'd have killed him had not Casey raised his hand.

With a smile of Christian charity great Casey's visage shone;

He stilled the rising tumult; he bade the game go on;

He signaled to the pitcher, and once more the spheroid flew;

But Casey still ignored it, and the umpire said, "Strike two."

"Fraud!" cried the maddened thousands, and echo answered fraud;

But one scornful look from Casey and the audience was awed.

They saw his face grow stern and cold, they saw his muscles strain,

And they knew that Casey wouldn't let that ball go by again.

The sneer is gone from Casey's lip, his teeth are clenched in hate;

He pounds with cruel violence his bat upon the plate.

And now the pitcher holds the ball, and now he lets it go,

And now the air is shattered by the force of Casey's blow.

Oh, somewhere in this favored land the sun is shining bright;

The band is playing somewhere, and somewhere hearts are light;

And somewhere men are laughing, and somewhere children shout;

But there is no joy in Mudville—mighty Casey has struck out.

Walt Disney's
The Ugly Dachshund

The Garrisons had three little dachshund pups—Chloe, Heidi, and Wilhelma—who were the favorites of Mrs. Garrison. And they had a fourth pup, who was the favorite of Mr. Garrison. His name was Brutus and he was a Great Dane. Poor Brutus! He thought he was a dachshund, too—a very large, clumsy, ugly dachshund.

Brutus grew and grew, as Great Dane pups always do. Soon, when Brutus stood on his hind legs, he was almost as tall as Mrs. Garrison. But he kept on thinking that he was a dachshund. He even ran the way dachshunds do—low and close to the ground.

Chloe, Heidi, and Wilhelma pattered into the house one day. Chloe grabbed a ball of wool in her mouth and ran. Heidi and Wilhelma chased her. Big Brutus lumbered after them, trying to join in the fun.

The ball unwound, and soon there was nothing but a mass of tangled wool.

The three dachshunds scampered off. But before poor Brutus could follow them, in came Mrs. Garrison. "Brutus!" she cried. "Look at what you've done!"

Another day, the three little dachshunds and Brutus raced into Mr. Garrison's art studio. Brutus knocked down a jar of paintbrushes, backed into a cabinet, and crashed into an enormous easel. When Mr. Garrison scolded him, poor Brutus whimpered sadly.

"Well, he's done it again," said Mrs. Garrison.

"Yes," said Mr. Garrison, "but after all, he's just a puppy."

"That's what worries me," said Mrs. Garrison. "What will he do when he gets bigger?"

Finally, Mr. Garrison was forced to put Brutus in an outdoor pen. After several whimpers, the pup settled down and closed his eyes.

Hours later, Brutus's eyes suddenly snapped open and he growled. Rising, he began to paw at the sides of the pen.

In the darkness, a strange man was coming toward the house. Brutus charged. In one big jump, he was out of the pen.

With a flying leap, he knocked down the stranger.

The stranger jumped to his feet and headed for a tree, with Brutus right behind him. The man swung himself up into the tree just in time. Brutus circled below, barking loudly.

Inside the house, the Garrisons thought that Brutus was barking because he was lonely. They turned over and went back to sleep.

Poor Brutus. It turned out that the strange man was a policeman who had been looking for prowlers. The Garrisons were sorry that the policeman had spent all night up in the tree. But Mr. Garrison was delighted that Brutus was such a good watchdog.

So Brutus stayed on with the Garrisons and the dachshunds. Before long, Brutus was no longer an oversized pup. He was a full-grown Great Dane—but he still thought he was a dachshund.

One night, the Garrisons had a party. Brutus was not invited. He was supposed to spend the evening in the backyard. Mrs. Garrison proudly showed Chloe to a guest. "She never gets into trouble the way Brutus does," she said.

Suddenly, there was an
unexpected guest at the party!
Brutus had managed to loosen his leash.
Barking his friendliest barks,
he came galloping
among the guests.
Chairs were soon
knocked over, tables
were toppled, and
the guests scattered.
The party was over.

Brutus was in disgrace. Even Mr. Garrison agreed that something had to be done. But the very next day, Brutus redeemed himself. Chloe fell into the garbage

can. When

the garbage

man came and

emptied the

trash—and

Chloe—into

his truck, Brutus barked and barked until the

Garrisons came out to rescue the little dachshund.

From then on, Mrs. Garrison no longer complained about Brutus, but she still thought he was a clumsy ox of a dog. So Mr. Garrison entered Brutus in an upcoming dog show. With the help of Doc Pruitt, a friendly kennel owner, Mr. Garrison taught Brutus to heel and stay. But there was still one thing Doc Pruitt couldn't figure out: "Why does he droop that way in the middle?" he asked.

"He still thinks he's a dachshund," Mr. Garrison said gloomily.

The day of the dog show soon arrived. When the Great Danes were called up, Mr. Garrison swallowed hard and led Brutus to the showring. And there, for the first time ever, Brutus saw other Great Danes! How tall and strong they were! How very handsome!

Brutus eyed the other Danes. Suddenly, he lifted his head proudly. At last he knew he was a Great Dane!

And can you guess which Great Dane won first prize that day. . . ?

It was Brutus! Mrs. Garrison was surprised and delighted.

There are still three little dachshunds living with the Garrisons. And with them lives a fourth dog of whom they're very proud. He is a huge and handsome Great Dane, and Brutus is his name.

Even when the road of life gets rocky, every heart has a way to make its dream come true. And that's exactly what John Henry believed. In fact, John Henry believed it so strongly that he laid down his very life for his dream.

John Henry and his dearest love, Polly, were born slaves. They didn't have a single thing to call their own. But all that changed when President Abraham Lincoln signed the Emancipation Proclamation, which freed all the slaves.

That's when John Henry vowed never to let his soul be chained again. He and Polly were married, and as a wedding present to her new husband, Polly had his slave chains forged into a mighty hammer. Then they set off together to find work and a place of their own.

In Talcott, West Virginia, John and Polly came upon a crew of workers laying new train track for the C&O Railroad. The railroad had promised fifty acres of land to every man who helped finish the line.

It was backbreaking work. It took the strength of three men to hammer in every steel spike that held the new track in place. To make matters worse, the railroad had moved up the crew's deadline.

"If we do not get to the other side of that mountain," said the foreman, "we can kiss our land good-bye!"

The workers were outraged. But John Henry confidently stepped forward with his hammer in his hand. "I'll take you there," he said, and he drove a spike into the ground with a single blow of his hammer.

The men looked on in amazement as John Henry went right to work, hammering in spike after spike,

 while Polly began to sing a work song to set the rhythm of their pace. The other men picked up their hammers and followed John's lead. Their spirits were lifted and their pace quickened.

As the work went on and the sound of John's hammer rang out, he met every challenge. John was an incredibly strong man. He could arm wrestle three men at once and beat them handily. He could drive a spike into a rock wall like a knife through butter.

Catching John Henry's spirit, the crew was soon back on schedule. The men felt that the dream of owning their own land was truly within their grasp. They took a break from their work to look down at the valley that would be their home when the job was done.

Then one morning, the crew's work was interrupted.

The ground vibrated as a large machine emerged from

a cloud of steam and came rolling up to the work site.

Workers scattered, but John stood to face the machine

as it rolled to a halt.

It was a steam drill, a new and powerful track-laying machine. The C&O Railroad had decided that a steam drill could finish the line faster than the men could.

"That thing's gonna take our jobs," said one of the workers.

The foreman came forward to confront the shadowy figure driving the steam drill. "But—but we had a contract!" said the foreman, holding out a piece of paper.

The driver took the paper and threw it into the smokestack of the steam drill.

At that, the angry workers charged the machine and tried to topple it. But John knew that wouldn't solve anything. He had an idea—a better way to settle things. He issued a challenge to the steam-drill driver: "I've got two free hands and a twenty-pound hammer. If I can beat this here machine, the land you promised is ours."

The driver tipped his hat in agreement, and the race was set to begin at once.

Polly rushed to John's side. "You don't have to do this," she said.

But John was determined. "Polly, if they steal our dreams, they put a chain  around our souls. Somebody's got to stand tall."

Polly turned away, knowing that once John had made up his mind, nothing could stand in his way.

The foreman stepped forward to announce the rules:

the winner of the challenge would be the one to drive in the most spikes by sundown. Then the foreman fired a pistol shot into the air, and the race was on!

It was man against machine. Side by side, John and the steam drill worked—one on one rail, one on the other, both hammering in spikes as fast as they could. John jumped out to an early lead, then fell behind as a gust of steam burst from the steam drill's smokestack. The machine doubled its speed.

Fueled by his dream, John Henry picked up his pace, too. His muscles strained. Sweat poured from his face. He swung his hammer over one shoulder and then over the other. Bit by bit, he not only caught up with the steam drill—he passed it!

And then — *thud* — John's hammer was halted in mid-swing. He looked up to find himself standing at the foot of a solid rock wall. The mountain! He had gone as far as he could go, and he had gotten there first. He had won the race! The crowd cheered.

But the race was not over yet. Behind John, the steam drill's engine continued to roar. A large, pointed hammer emerged from the front of the machine and began to pound its way into the solid rock. The steam drill was going to cut a hole clear through the mountain!

John Henry sank to one knee and dropped his

hammer. How could flesh and blood compete with

wheels and gears?

But Polly went

to John, handed

his hammer back

to him, and

encouraged him

to go on. A fellow

railroad worker threw John a second hammer. They

knew John's strength. They knew John's determination.

They knew John could do it.

In his own heart, John knew he could do it, too. Slowly, he drew

himself up. He held the hammers above his head and smashed them against the mountain. With a hammer in each hand, his arms became a windmill of power. Rocks and boulders flew everywhere, and John Henry dug his way into the mountainside.

Inside the mountain, sparks from the steam drill and the red-hot trails of John's hammers lit up the darkness. The earth shook as the two giants battled their way through the rock.

Meanwhile, Polly and the railroad workers waited on the other side of the mountain to see who would come out first.

Finally, with an explosion of rock and dust, a powerful force broke through. As the dust cleared, the crowd strained to see. Yes! It was John Henry! He raised his hammers high into the air just as the sun set in the west.

John had done it. But something was not right.

John's chest heaved, and he collapsed to his knees.

Polly rushed to him and caught him as he fell back into

her arms. John Henry

had given every ounce

of strength he had to

give.

Years later, Polly

would show her son,

John Henry, Jr., a story

quilt that told of his legendary papa—about his

strength, about his determination, about the way that even as he breathed his last breath, he was smiling: "'Cause he moved that mountain and led us to the promised land," she would say. "You can move mountains, too, baby. All you gotta do is believe."

WALT DISNEY's
TOBY TYLER

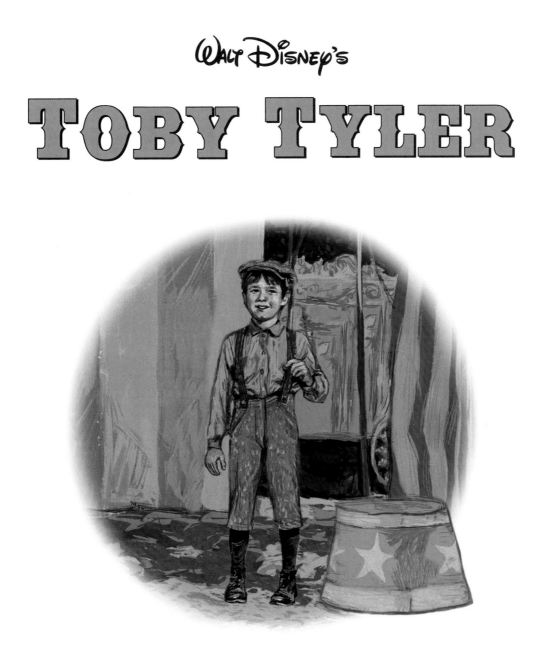

* * * ⭐ * * *

Toby Tyler wished he could buy a ticket to Colonel Castle's Great American Circus. But how could he? He had only a penny in his pocket.

"Crispy, crunchy, circus peanuts!" called the peanut vendor.

Toby said, "How many for a penny?"

Mr. Tupper, the peanut vendor, gave him six big ones.

"Would you care to join the circus?" said Mr. Tupper. "I need a helper."

Toby thought that would be better than anything in the world. "But my uncle needs me on the farm," he said. "Thanks, anyway."

When Toby got back to the farm, his uncle was angry. "Toby, you forgot to feed the hogs," he said. "The hungry hogs broke down the fence around their pen. They rooted up all the turnips."

"Now we have no turnip crop to sell," said Aunt Olive. She looked sad.

Toby had to show his uncle and aunt how sorry he was. Suddenly, he knew what he would do. He would earn money to pay for the ruined crop. That night, when everyone was asleep, Toby packed up his things and crept outside. He was going to join the circus!

He became Mr. Tupper's helper. His job was to carry a tray about and call out, "Peanuts? Peanuts and taffy apples!"

Toby had lots of customers. But there was one who

never paid—a hungry circus monkey who snatched a nut or an apple every time Toby came by.

There was so much to see at Colonel Castle's Great American Circus! There was Mighty Benjo, the strong man. There was Sam Treat, the clown. And there were those daring young bareback riders—Jeanette and Ajax. Sometimes Toby watched the show and forgot to sell peanuts and taffy apples.

One day, Toby

even put down his tray to watch. He did not see the monkeyshines going on behind his back! Poor Toby had to pay for everything the naughty monkey ate.

Poor monkey! What a stomachache he had. When Toby saw how sick the stubby little monkey was, he felt sorry for him. He gave him medicine and nursed him back to health.

"I'll call you Mr. Stubbs," said Toby. "And we'll be friends."

After that, Toby and Mr. Stubbs were always together.

Weeks and months passed. Toby worked hard, saved up lots of money, and wrote to his uncle to say he would be home soon. But then one night, while Toby slept and the circus caravan rolled through the night, Mr. Stubbs threw Toby's money away! It was as if Mr. Stubbs wanted Toby to stay with the circus forever.

The next morning, Toby figured out what had happened. He asked Mr. Stubbs why he

had thrown the money away. The monkey could only chatter with fright. He did not understand why Toby was so angry. He wished his friend would smile at him.

Just then, there was a call for help from the practice ring!

Ajax, the bareback rider, had hurt his leg. "Now who will ride with Jeanette?" said Colonel Castle. "We have a big show next week."

"Let me try!" said Toby. "I rode my uncle's horse many times."

But *doing tricks* on a horse was another matter. Could Mighty Benjo and Sam Treat make a bareback rider of Toby in just one week? Day and night they worked with Toby in the practice ring. Toby had no time that week to play with Mr. Stubbs. Poor Mr. Stubbs thought his friend was still angry.

Before Toby knew it, the night of the big show arrived. Colonel Castle announced the bareback-riding act, and Jeanette and Toby ran into the ring and landed on the horses' backs with flying leaps.

The band played a waltz, and the horses moved slowly around the ring.

Mighty Benjo said, "So far, so good."

But there were more difficult tricks to come. At the end of the act, Toby had to jump through a flaming hoop.

The hoops were in place. The band played faster. The horses cantered faster. Then Jeanette and Toby, standing on their horses' backs,

jumped through the flames. . . .

Out they came on the other side of the hoop and landed gracefully on their horses!

Mr. Stubbs chattered happily. His friend was smiling again. Toby wasn't angry anymore. Mr. Stubbs leaped into the ring and up onto Toby's horse. Everybody cheered and clapped for the daring young bareback riders and for the happy monkey!

After that, Toby had enough money to pay for the turnip crop. So he said good-bye to the circus and went home. But he never forgot his circus days. How could he? His friend, Mr. Stubbs, was always nearby, getting into mischief.

Walt Disney's
MICKEY MOUSE'S PICNIC

Mickey was very happy. It was a lovely afternoon, and he and Minnie were going on a picnic with their friends. Mickey peeked inside the picnic basket Minnie had packed. Yum! There were peanut-butter-and-jelly sandwiches, cold-meat sandwiches, deviled eggs

and potato salad, radishes and onions, pink lemonade, and a big chocolate cake!

Mickey picked up the basket, and he and Minnie went out to the car, where Pluto, Goofy, Daisy Duck, and Clarabelle Cow were waiting for them.

"It seems strange to go without Donald Duck," said Mickey as they drove away.

"Yes," said Minnie, "but there is always trouble when Donald is along."

None of them saw Donald watching them leave.

Everyone sang merrily as Mickey drove down the road to the picnic grounds. It was a perfect day for a picnic. First they went for a walk along the riverbank. Then they found a grassy spot beneath a tall tree. They left the picnic basket there while they went for a swim in the swimming hole.

How good that fresh, cool water felt! They swam and floated and played around, and had a wonderful time. But afterward, when they

returned to their grassy spot, their picnic lunch was gone! "We'll soon find out about this!" Mickey cried. They searched all over

the picnic grounds without seeing a sign of the picnic basket. At last, they came out on the road, near the spot where they had left Mickey's car.

It was then that they met Donald Duck, walking down the road. He had a fishing pole over one shoulder. A bundle hung from the end of the fishing pole.

"Imagine meeting you folks out here," said Donald. "I came to do some fishing. Got tired of spending a lonely day at home."

"Oh—er—yes," said Mickey. He felt bad because they had left Donald behind.

"Where are you folks going?" Donald asked.

"We are hunting for our lunch," Mickey said.

"Lunch?" said Donald. "Why, I have enough

for us all in my bundle here."

Now everyone felt guilty. But they were hungry, so they said thank you and accepted Donald's invitation.

Donald opened his bundle and spread out his lunch. Yum! There were peanut-butter-and-jelly sandwiches, cold-meat sandwiches, deviled eggs and potato salad, radishes and onions, pink lemonade, and a big chocolate cake!

Mickey threw Minnie a puzzled look when he saw the contents of the picnic lunch.

Minnie turned to Donald and flashed her sweetest smile. "Did you bring a knife for cutting the cake, Donald?" she asked.

"Er—I had one somewhere," Donald said, searching around.

"I taped a knife to the bottom of *my* cake plate," Minnie said.

Mickey leaned over and peeked at the bottom of the cake plate. Sure enough, there was a knife taped to it. On the knife handle were the initials "M.M."

"So, that's where our picnic lunch disappeared to!" cried Mickey.

Donald looked at his feet. "I'm sorry," he said. "I won't ever do it again."

"And where is my lunch basket?" Minnie asked.

"In the back of Mickey's car," Donald admitted.

Mickey finally had to laugh. "I think we've all learned a lesson," he said.

"Donald won't snatch any more picnic baskets, and we know it's better to bring Donald on a picnic."

And when they were finished with their lunch, they all piled back into Mickey's car. They even made room for Donald . . . in the empty picnic basket.

Walt Disney's
Pollyanna

Pollyanna stared around her new room. "I'm glad there isn't a mirror," she said to Nancy, the maid. "I won't have to look at my freckles. I'm  glad, too, to have a room of my very own."

"Do you always find something to be glad about?" asked Nancy.

"I try to," said Pollyanna. She was an orphan. She had just come to live with her rich Aunt Polly. Aunt Polly was very strict, but she was good to Pollyanna and bought her many lovely new clothes. Pollyanna had never owned any brand-new clothes—only hand-me-downs.

One morning, Pollyanna was walking by the orphanage when she saw a boy climbing out of a window. He swung into a tree, then jumped neatly down to the sidewalk.

"I'm Jimmy Bean," he said to Pollyanna. "I'm an orphan."

"So am I," said Pollyanna. "My name is Pollyanna Whittier."

"I'm going fishing," said Jimmy. "Do you want to come along?"

Pollyanna nodded, and away they went to

the stream. They had no hook. Instead, they used a tin can tied to a string. They did not catch a single fish, but they had fun.

On the way home, Jimmy took Pollyanna into a big, overgrown garden. He pointed to a tree in front of a big house. "This is the tallest tree in town," he said. "Be very quiet. Old Man Pendergast lives here, and he hates kids."

Pollyanna was a little scared, but she followed Jimmy over to the tree.

"I'm going to climb the tree," said Jimmy. "I bet I can see the whole town from the top." He started to shinny up the trunk

when —*crash!*— a wild-eyed old man burst out of the underbrush. It was Pendergast!

Pendergast tried to grab Pollyanna, but she ducked

out of his reach. Jimmy was not so lucky. Pendergast

seized him and dragged him into the house.

"Help!" screamed Jimmy.

Pollyanna wanted to run away. But Jimmy was her friend. She had to try to help him. Bravely, she headed into the house. Pendergast and Jimmy were in the living room. The old

man was about to telephone the police.

"You let Jimmy go!" Pollyanna said loudly. "He didn't hurt anything, and neither did I."

Pendergast was so surprised that he let go of the boy. Jimmy dashed for the door, and disappeared quickly before the old man could catch him.

Pendergast glared at Pollyanna. "Go on. Get out of here!" he bellowed.

Pollyanna started to go, then stopped short. On the wall were beautiful patches of colored light.

"What a beautiful rainbow!" she said with a gasp.

"That's not a rainbow," hissed Pendergast. "It's the sun shining through the prisms of the lamp."

"I like to think it's a rainbow," said Pollyanna. Then she added, "Maybe you're not glad I came here, but I am." And she skipped merrily out of the room.

One day, the townspeople decided to hold a big fair to raise money for a new orphanage. Pollyanna did all she could to help. She even asked Old Man Pendergast to take a booth and sell glass pendants.

"We'll call them rainbow-makers," said Pollyanna.

But when Aunt Polly found out about the fair, she forbade Pollyanna to go. She thought the old orphanage should be repaired instead of having a new one built.

Pollyanna tried to change Aunt Polly's mind about the fair. "But they're going to have a parade—"

"You're not going, and that's the end of it!" snapped Aunt Polly.

But Pollyanna did go. Jimmy Bean helped her climb down the big tree outside her attic window. They were so quiet, Aunt Polly did not hear them.

At the fair, Pollyanna and Jimmy ate ice cream, watermelon, taffy apples, and corn on the cob. And Pollyanna pulled a beautiful doll out of the fishpond booth.

"Am I glad!" she cried. "I never had a doll of my own before!"

When Pollyanna got home, she climbed back up the tree easily. But as she jumped over to the windowsill, she slipped and fell to the ground.

Aunt Polly heard Pollyanna scream and hurried outside.

Pollyanna was lying very, very still.

"She is badly hurt," Aunt Polly told Nancy. "Call Dr. Chilton! And hurry!"

The next day, Dr. Chilton told Pollyanna that her legs had been hurt, and that she had to go to the hospital.

"I won't go," said Pollyanna. "I'll never get well. And I'll never be glad again in my whole life, either."

Aunt Polly was sad when she heard this. She loved Pollyanna very much—and she was not the only one. Pollyanna had won the love of everyone in town. That afternoon, they all came to see her, including Jimmy and Pendergast.

"Mr. Pendergast's adopted me," said Jimmy.

"Oh, I'm so glad!" cried Pollyanna. She thought for a moment. Then she smiled. "I *will* go to the hospital, Aunt Polly—and I'll get well for you and all my friends."

And she did!

The Little House

* * * ★ * * *

Once upon a time, there was a little house on a little hill, way out in the country. She was a happy little house, for she loved the country life — the peace and quiet, the warm sun on her roof, and the whisper of the summer breeze 'round her eaves.

One day,
a young
couple, just
married,
pulled up to
the little

house in a horse and buggy. The bride took one look at

the little house and hugged the groom in delight, while

the little house blushed with pride. And as the young

couple crossed over the threshold together, the little

house became a home.

As time passed, the young couple had children, and the family grew and grew. The little house felt blessed to be the one to provide them with warmth and shelter. She was surrounded daily by the sound of laughter as the children played in and around her. Of course,

children at play are not always careful and gentle, and the little house suffered the occasional broken window and damaged shingle.

But these little pains—even broken panes—were soon forgotten.

It was only at night that the little house felt just a little bit lonely. She wondered what it would be like to have other houses around to talk to. Then she would gaze wistfully toward the distant lights of the city, never realizing that all the time, those lights were

coming closer and closer. Rows of houses and street lamps were springing up almost overnight as the city grew larger and larger, its reach extending further and further into the surrounding countryside.

Before long, the little house had two new neighbors on either side of her: two lovely and stately Victorian mansions.

What perfectly elegant neighbors, thought the little house. Why, I'm right in the very center of the social world.

Music from grand dinner parties drifted out the windows of one of the mansions, but when the little

house hummed along, she received only scornful looks from the superior Victorians.

Land sakes! thought the little house. I was only trying to be neighborly.

Then one night, one of the mansions caught fire. "Help! Help!" screamed the mansion. "Sound the alarm!"

The fire department arrived in minutes, but not before the fire had spread and ignited part of the little house's roof, as well as the mansion on the other side of her. At last, the water from the fire hoses put out the flames. But when the smoke and steam had cleared, the little house saw that both mansions had burned down.

My, my, thought the little house. What a pity.

The years rolled by faster now, and the little house saw the dawn of a new century. The tempo of life had

quickened. Everything was bigger and better. This was the age of progress. The little house looked up at the apartment buildings towering over her on all sides and thought, Here I am, completely surrounded by progress.

Unfortunately, her family did not like their new situation, smack-dab in the middle of so much hustle and bustle. So they packed up their things and moved away.

If only I could go with them, thought the little house. But, of course, she couldn't. Come what may, she had to stand her ground.

And so she did, even when the wrecking ball eventually came to demolish the neighboring apartment buildings. The little house tried to look on the bright side. Well, if there's one thing about progress, she thought, it always progresses. Maybe now, she thought, she could have a little peace.

But almost immediately, new buildings began to go up around the little house. This time, they were not apartment buildings, but office buildings . . . skyscrapers! Steel beams were laid, one on top of the other, by giant cranes. The sky was the limit.

Meanwhile, far below, in the dark shadow of the skyscrapers, the little house wondered, What's to become of me? Will I never feel the sun again, or feel the gentle touch of the summer breeze, or hear the song of the meadowlark?

Poor forgotten little house. There was nothing left now—not even hope. And so, when the wrecking and moving company came for her, with tools and trucks and chains, the little house decided it was just as well. I'm just in the way, she thought. I'm no good to anybody. And we all have to go sometime.

The little house could not watch, but she felt the workers wrench her up off her foundation. She felt herself being moved and loaded onto a truck. She felt herself being chained down and hauled away—perhaps to the city dump, she thought.

But then the little house felt the sun on her face, she felt the gentle touch of the

breeze, and she thought she heard the song of the meadow-lark. But how could that be? The little house opened her eyes to find that she had not been thrown away—she had been moved out of the city and into the countryside! It wasn't the end, after all. It was just the beginning.

Oh, it took a little time and a lot of fixing, but what really mattered is that she had been found by someone who would love and cherish her — someone who knew that the best place to find peace and happiness is in a little house on a little hill, way out in the country.

Walt Disney's
The Brave Engineer

It was another early morning at the railroad yard, and most of the train engineers were still sound asleep. But not Casey Jones. Just like clockwork, Casey Jones was ready to climb aboard his locomotive and head out west to deliver his precious cargo.

Just what was so precious about it, you might ask?
Why, it was the U.S. Mail! Casey knew that folks
depended on their mail—especially those who lived
way out in the west. Nothing was more important to
Casey than delivering the mail on time.

So, with the mailbag loaded onto the train, Casey Jones was off, and right on schedule, too. Yes, the weather was fine, the engine was purring, and there was clear track ahead as far as the eye could see.

The train rolled through the countryside, mile after mile, and Casey sat back, put up his feet, and settled in for a smooth journey. It was going so well that Casey even had time to get choosy with the pieces of coal that were going into the furnace.

But over the next hill, everything changed. The weather turned stormy, the rain poured down, and before long, Casey's train was ten feet deep in floodwater!

What was Casey Jones to do? The mail had to get through! So good old Casey drove his train on through the flood, climbed onto the roof, and started to paddle.

Hours later, Casey brought that train through the flood and out onto dry track on the other side. But the damage had been done. Casey Jones was running late! He shoveled more coal into the furnace and doubled the train's speed. He had to make up for lost time.

A few miles down the track and around a bend, Casey approached another obstacle. A sneering villain had tied up a fair damsel and laid her across the tracks

in Casey's path! How could Casey save her without losing more time?

Brave Casey Jones climbed

out of the racing locomotive and onto the cowcatcher

at the front of the train. Then, just as the train reached

the damsel, Casey leaned over, scooped her gently off

the tracks, and carried her inside the locomotive. What

a hero! Why, Casey even dropped her off safely at the

next station before racing on into the mountains.

But Casey's heroics hadn't gained him any time. He was still running late! He shoveled more coal into the furnace and cranked up the train's speed. If he could keep up the pace, thought Casey, he might have a chance at getting the mail through on time.

What Casey couldn't see was that a mysterious man was up to no good about a mile down the tracks. In the shadows of the mountains, the mysterious man laughed wickedly as he placed a bundle of dynamite on a railroad bridge and lit the fuses.

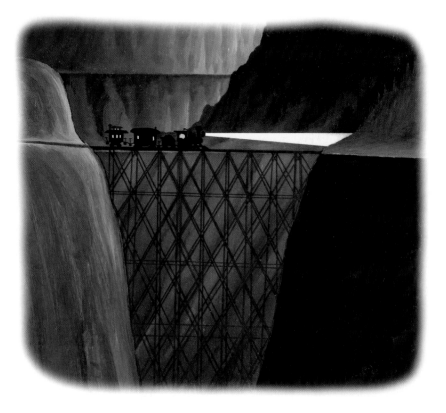

Poor Casey Jones! He had no idea what was in store for him as his train wound its way through the mountain pass and raced onto the bridge. Halfway across—*kaboom!*—the dynamite exploded, the bridge gave way, and Casey's train tumbled into the dark canyon.

Now, for a lesser engineer, that might have been the end of the story. But Casey Jones just fired up that train engine and steered her straight up the canyon wall. Oh, it took some straining, but eventually Casey Jones had that train out of the canyon and back on track.

Casey might have been back on track, but he was not back on schedule. In fact, now Casey was *really* late. So, he shoveled pile after pile of coal into the furnace, pushing the engine harder than ever. Casey was so busy shoveling that it took him a while to see the gang of bandits who had climbed aboard his train.

Well, Casey Jones had not come this far and worked so hard just to be derailed by a few bandits!

And besides, thought Casey, who did they think they were, invading *his* locomotive? Casey Jones used his coal shovel to fend off the bandits and managed to knock them all off the train.

Furiously, Casey Jones shoveled coal into the furnace until it was full to bursting. Thick black smoke poured out of the smokestack. The train barreled down the track at lightning speed.

Casey frantically worked the controls, trying to get every last ounce of power out of his machine. And just

when it seemed that nothing could stop brave Casey Jones and his mighty engine, Casey turned to look down the track . . .

. . . and saw another train hurtling toward him from the opposite direction.

The men
on the other
train managed
to jump clear
before the
two trains
collided in a

tremendous wreck. But not Casey Jones.

Was this the end of the line for the brave engineer?

Hours later, out west, the station clerk checked his watch. Casey Jones was ten minutes late. It was so unlike Casey to be late that the clerk doubted he was coming at all. Sadly, the clerk shuffled over to the ARRIVALS board and raised his hand to erase Casey's name. Suddenly, he heard the distant sound of a train whistle. Could it be?

A battered locomotive limped into the station carrying a bruised Casey Jones. And do you know what Casey was clutching in his arms?

Yes, it was the mailbag. It hadn't been easy, but

Casey Jones had done his duty. When all was said and done, he had gotten the mail through on time. Well—almost.

Collect All of Your Favorite Disney Tales in These Beautifully Illustrated and Gilded Storybook Volumes!

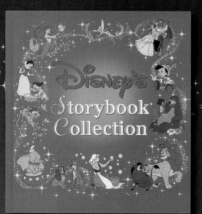

$15.99 Each

(CAN $19.99)

Available at your local bookstore

Be sure to visit
www.disneybooks.com